Tales of
Love & Parasites

By Javier Bonafont

Contents

Preface

This is the first collection of stories I have let loose onto the world. I know they are not for everybody, but if they are out there, inhabiting many heads, then they no longer have to lurk exclusively in my head, and I can maybe have some peace. Perhaps this is selfish.

Hemispheres

My lids droop. I am a canvas sack of stones and sand yearning for the earth. I close my eyes. I accept the darkness, the sleep, whatever may come. I hope for something terrible. Something unexpectedly terminal to bring it all to a close and empty me into the ground.

I've ached in my heart for you for a long time. Its possible you know.

But I move at the speed of humans. Neurons fire at the speed of light. And I have an enemy brain.

A deathstar to my X-wing, my enemy brain outguns me a millionfold. It rearranges the past and surges effortlessly to the future. Everything I would do, it does first, better, faster, and then is instantly yawning and restless. A rabbit to my turtle, I am as if a stone monument to stillness. I think to put in an old Tom

Waits cd, but before I can make a move, before I can even think of where to reach for it, my enemy brain has played it in my head. It has already listened, its already happened. I lose again.

At times I distract it. Sometimes a bottle of wine confuses it, sends it chasing up quixotic mobius loops, letting me act. Real moments are created in those sparing gaps. But wine confounds us all equally, makes those moments of dubious taste or value. Even so, they are unalterably real and mine.

Which is a lie I tell myself. Were real only once. Are actual only fleetingly, become memories too quickly, become hostage to the adversary in my skull who rules past and future. And once there, the altering begins. Never ends, becomes a disfigured mockery.

In what sense have "we" been to the moon? Asks my enemy brain. I have no answer.

My enemy brain has been not only satisfied, it has been satisfied with a you that can never really have existed, the one that finds me electrically exhilarating and an infinite feast, and yet, for all that, is herself a disillusionment. Perhaps because of that she is a disillusionment. I cannot be what I have made myself have to be.

In its circular time, the dog is delighted and surprised every day to see the sun rise. But the you of my mind will never leave me. I am responsible for her now. All I can do is disappoint and hurt her. I can ache, then, and nothing more.

Its been too long, my eyes flick-flick open. But there is no onrushing truck, no deadly precipice, no barricaded bridge. Just the straight empty road relentlessly streaming past. I've veered but an inch from the center of the lane. It all continues.

The Final Letter
of Dr. Morris Stanley

(Reprinted by permission from Science Fact and Fiction Quarterly)

Dear Readers,

As a writer of hard science stories well known to you on these pages, you surely know by now that I do not dabble in fantasy, ghost tales nor any of that paranormal nonsense currently in vogue. So when some months ago I came into the possession of a small box of letters from my great aunt Abigail, and happened across one impossibly odd bit of correspondence, I tried for a good deal of time to figure if I was in some way able to spin a yarn from it. But in the end, I know my limits. I write of orbits and thrusts, nuts and bolts, and this was quite beyond that. Sure it has machines and scientists in it, but I could not begin to fashion a story from it that could ever exceed the original text. So with due respect to my dearly departed great aunt and the mysterious Dr. Stanley, whomever he might have been, I re-print this, his final letter, here in its entirety.

Within an envelope labeled "Please deliver to Miss Abigail Phelps, Number 21 Dorset Way, Bournemouth, England" was the following:

July 10, 1903.

Dearest Abigail and Whomever Else It Might Concern:

I write this from what is likely to be my final repose in a small cellar workspace beneath the apparatus storage facility of Nancy-Université. Alone now for what I realize is the first time in my life, there is in my mind a bewildering clarity and expansiveness to my thoughts. Perhaps this is the clarity that leads to brilliance in such minds as Poincaré or Tesla. If only I had time, this would be a line of investigation: whether the great minds of our time are perchance those few fortunate individuals to not be burdened by the debilitating effects of succubotic fiends. But I cannot digress, my time is short. They circle outside, awaiting a safe entry. If fortune be on my side, I will have been long dead by then. The constant exposure to the emanations of the Crooke's Tubes has turned my skin a painful raw red, and my vision grows more blurred by the minute. I am quite simply being baked by an invisible heat, but it has afforded me these few moments of liberty with which to relate the events of the past few days. The dynamo powering the apparatus will no doubt run out of fuel soon, so I can only pray it last long enough to ensure my demise.

Where to begin? With the abominations themselves? Or instead, better perhaps detail the events in order of occurrence. To speak of the results without the background would lead you, with justification, to dismiss my writings as that of a fool or the hallucinations of a man whose brain has been boiled by the relentless fury of the Rayos-X. I am neither fool nor suffering dementia, and what I must relate is of such import as cannot be overstated and is very much real, although in what manner of the word real I mean cannot be easily formulated, as will be evident presently.

The entire tale first begins with my apprenticeship at the 5th Avenue workshop of the remarkable Mr. Nikolai Tesla in the year 1891. At the time he was immersed in the field of wireless transmissions of energy and it was then that the idea of observing the paths of energies through the trans-ether was broached. Mister Tesla was, however, a practical scientist, and did not so much care for observing phenomena as much as harnessing it. So the work of developing what came to be known as the Ether-Scopic Spectacles was entrusted to me, and soon he put it out of his mind entirely.

That is not to say that he had no hand in it, quite the contrary. For Mr. Tesla's initial insights into the problem were of such lucidity that the whole path of my endeavor was plainly laid out. Without his astute dissection of the electro-mechanical requirements the device would need to fulfill, I would likely have thrashed about for years and given up on the task. Even more important than his keen practical guidance at the outset was his offhand confidence that a solution was not only possible, but so lacking in challenge that a lowly apprentice such as I could carry it to completion. Buttressed by the knowledge that Tesla knew it could be done, I had no doubts that I would succeed. Even after the fire in 1895 forced him to release me and others from his employ, I soldiered on with the project for the next eight years on my own.

Indeed the developing of the Spectacles took a good deal more time and effort than anticipated, especially when I no longer had the luxury of Tesla's workshop in which to operate. Sadly, I confess that owing either to a fault in my mathematics, or a limitation in my design and construction, the Ether-Scopic Spectacles have never yet succeeded in detecting the electro field paths we had set out to observe, and while the professor will likely never know of it, I find in these last hours that being robbed of life means I shall never complete that work which he entrusted to me. This fills me with a profound sense of disappointment that I cannot fully understand, considering the circumstances, but he remains at this last moment the one person who I desired to impress with my abilities, and who, if he were here, could have provided some hope to our present difficulties. Had I succeeded, had I been able to present to him a working prototype, then perhaps he would have been a part of the most unfortunate turn of events that was to follow.

What followed instead was an intersection of my work with that of the Frenchman Prosper-René Blondlot. Blondlot was no charlatan, for he had obtained significant fame in work on the speed and nature of electromagnetics and radio waves, and after a chance encounter he invited me to his laboratory at the Nancy-Université to assist him and concurrently continue my work on the Spectacles. But if he was no poseur, neither was Dr. Blondlot a Tesla, which was soon evident. His current fascination was with the uses of the device called a Crooke's Tube, which expelled the so-called Rayos-X, or "X-ray" which could not be seen by the naked eye but caused effects at a distance. These very devices are to be the proximate cause of my end soon, but at the time I began working with them they were quite marvelous, capable of penetrating matter as if it did not exist.

There were a great variety of the emanators, and it became my purpose to investigate if the spectacles would be capable of observing the transmission paths of their energies through space. It should be noted that I continue to utilize the term "spectacles" despite the true nature of the mechanism I had created, which is the size of an Edison Kinetoscope on steel casters with a glass viewplate coated with a formulation of phosphoric powders that Tesla had procured for the project. My implementation of it was undoubtedly crude and inelegant, and had thus far failed to display any images whatsoever. The tests with the Crooke's Tubes were likewise singular failures with regard to the machine's designated purpose.

Failure, however, cannot begin to describe the monumental calamity that befell us that day. After the initial tests revealed nothing on the spectacle's screen, Blondlot wished to confirm that the tubes were in fact emitting so he crossed to the other end of the room to see if his detector was confirming the Rayos. It was at the moment he moved across the field of the Rayos that the spectacle's window plate lit up for the very first time. I shouted at Blondlot to be still, and moved the cabinet toward him. The more I aligned the view, however, the more blank with confusion I became at what I observed.

The glowing figure I witnessed was not, as I had imagined, a radiant version of Blondlot. It was not even remotely a human shape, nor was it even touching the ground. While it floated roughly in the same general area as Blondlot, it was clearly not he. Upon examination it seemed not so much suspended in the air as clinging to the place Blondlot was occupying. As this sounds confusing, I will elaborate as to what I perceived. Through my naked eyes I could see Blondlot, standing impatiently in the center of the testing area. On the Spectacle's observation screen I could see a glowing mass that hovered in the air. If I combined these two images in my mind, it appeared that the glowing mass was positioned on the back and neck of the professor, as would be an overlarge packsack worn by a Himalayan Sherpa.

The next few moments was a farcical attempt by me to keep the irritated professor from moving without revealing to him what I was observing, for I was myself growing more and more alarmed. What I began to discern as I moved the machine about and closer was that this was not just a shapeless glow, but something of an abhorrence so beyond comprehension that it left me completely without words as I examined it.

It moved. More precisely, it pulsed like a grotesquely enormous heart. This was without a doubt a living creature, a horrible tangle of translucent life. Shapeless in the way of an octopus; it possessed an array of tentacles and a mass of finer tendrils too numerous to count that could be seen writhing gruesomely in and through all parts of Blondlot. I stepped forward and hesitantly ran my hand across Blondlot's back. I felt nothing but the hairs on my arm standing on end with disgust. The hideous cephalopod I could see on the glass plate could neither be seen nor felt with normal human senses.

The patience of the professor had by this point been entirely exhausted and he demanded to know what I was carrying on about with such rapt attention. How could I explain what I was seeing? Moving the machine to a final view, I could see this monstrous parasite unmistakably had an enormous proboscis coming out of its headlike region and plunging into the center of Blondlot's brain, sucking and draining his very head with a steady throb. It was not something one admitted saying aloud. It was all I could do to keep from screaming at the sight and smashing the instrument. But the conundrum was obvious: it was simply not possible for the professor to be both in front of the screen and behind it, I could not show him what I saw without constructing some elaborate set of mirrors and optics.

What occurred to me next was such that I felt for certain I would lose my intestinal fortitude. For I volunteered then to have Blondlot go behind the machine and observe my body as it stood in the path of the Rayos-X. Even as I said it, even as Blondlot was cursing my evasiveness, I knew in my heart what was to come. The gasp of horror from the professor only confirmed the sickening feeling that washed over me. I could see in his face what I now felt was the throbbing sucking sensation in my skull. I could now feel with every breath the gentle resistance of the tendrils and tentacles that were sunk deeply into my limbs and organs. I would have sworn then that I could feel the creature's breath on my neck. A mere few minutes prior

I had never conceived of anything so foul as what I now felt, and only seconds prior I had imagined that I had discovered a rare, in fact singular, demon or fiend that had accursed my friend. But the true wave of revulsion that came over me now was the realization that this was not a rare or singular event. I came to know at once that not only did I harbor one of the fiends also, but that I had carried this insubstantial succubus upon and within me for all the time I could recall.

After a brief exchange wherein Blondlot accused me of trickery and childish pranks, the professor accepted what his eyes revealed to him, and we took turns in front of the machine comparing observations and drawings of what we saw. We concluded quite quickly that whatever it was that afflicted us was not corporeal in any sense we understood but a being of the ether and that exposure to the Rayos-X made them visible to the spectacles but that no interaction with them seemed possible. The professor suggested, rather spuriously, that the succubi were creatures of electro-magnetic origin and hence were emitting a detectable radio field he later called "N-Rays" and that the Rayos-X were amplifying an existing energy from the monster. I note this only to say I saw no reasoning behind this conjecture, and that it was not in any way supported by the evidence we collected. As the professor will now most assuredly be the one who advances this research, I felt it necessary to state my views in the time I have left.

Over the next two days we paraded ninety-two unsuspecting individuals from the university and local area in front of the device. We revealed nothing to the subjects, neither before nor after, but in every instance we observed a succubus parasite upon them in much the same manner of ours. In a child as young as five and an elderly groundskeeper of sixty-four we observed the identical results. We observed also that the succubi possessed fainter tendrils that extended outward from them to unknown lengths, and we surmised that these tendrils, being not of matter but of an ethereal force, could, like a beam of light or a radio signal, be limitless miles long. We further observed that these tendrils may be connected to other fiends, as perhaps may belong to a group or, and I hesitate to use so affecting a term, perchance "families" of parasites. In one instance we lured to the experiment a visiting professor and his new paramour, and when they stood before the machine we noted that the parasites were entangled with tendrils. No matter how far away the two stood, the tendrils stretched effortlessly between them. The lovers were conjoined more than they could realize, and that led me to wonder later which of the two events led to the other. Was the attraction between these two people a cause, or a result of the entangling tendrils of their succubus? If the latter, was all our so-called free will to be called into question?

Finally, and fatefully, we discovered that succubi did not enjoy the Rayos-X. If a body was placed in close proximity to an emanator the Succubus would separate from its host. Not fully and entirely, for small trace tendrils stretched to the gelatinous mass, but it would hover for the most part a discrete distance from the Rayos. When the subject moved away from the emanator, or the power of the Crooke's tube was turned down, the parasite would drift back and plunge its tentacles back into the host.

This presented a problem in our continuing observations, for we desired more intensity in order to see more clearly the details of the succubus. So for an entire day I worked upon varying the emanations from the various Crooke's mechanisms to see if there was any wavelength that would cast light as it were, without pushing away the parasite. In this endeavor I unfortunately succeeded. In the experiment logs, the final notation was for the tube I had labeled "Bernhardt:" (in reference to its oddly temperamental nature). The modifications to Bernhardt are noted in the log. I recall doing six variants. The last one noted was successful. There were no further modifications or attempts beyond that, for reasons that shall be abundantly clear.

The Bernhardt emanator, when aimed at the body of a volunteer, despite being as invisible to the human eye as all the other Rayo tubes, succeeded in illuminating the succubus like an arc light. It was an unqualified success as a tool to observe the succubus. But immediately I recognized the unforeseen error. At the very moment the foul creature was struck by the rays, it did something I had not yet ever seen, for it immediately turned its misshapen, eyeless head and faced me, as if noticing my existence for the first time.

While this instilled a degree of panic in me, I was still capable of making an observation, and it was this: upon affixing me with its eyeless gaze, it simultaneously plunged an entire new growth of tendrils into the brain of the subject. This seemed to affect the subject to a marked degree, insofar as the young man immediately began to protest that he no longer wished to be a part of the experiment. But beyond that, while watching the sudden ingestion of new probing tentacles, I realized that I was feeling that same effect in my own head and I felt myself thinking to myself that I was a threat, that I was in need of being eradicated. With great difficulty I was able to form other thoughts at the same time as this, but in the manner of reasoning through a dense fog. I pieced together slowly the fact that this thought in my head was not my own, but that of the parasite, that it was the one feeling the threat. I could feel my own creature suckling at my mind, reacting to his sibling's sudden knowledge of what I had witnessed of them.

I was plainly discovered. My own brain would freely vomit up its contents to the sucking proboscis sunk deep into my grey organ. And worse, I felt more horrible things being pumped into me as my memories of the past days were purged out. I felt at once a sudden and complete horror for what I had done and a plan crystallized quickly. It was, for a moment, without question whatsoever that I would have to find and kill Professor Blondlot, for he was the one that had brought this ruin upon us all. This thought was topmost in my mind as I set about thinking where he would be at this moment and what weapon I could use. As I searched the laboratory for a suitable object to shatter his skull, I unintentionally stood directly before a fully powered Crooke's tube and I felt a wave of confusion.

Why had I been searching for an instrument to attack Blondlot? That was senseless. Of course, it was only senseless to me. Not to the parasites, and the momentary flight my creature took away from the burning emanator gave me the opportunity to clear my thoughts long enough to realize what I had to do. Within a minute's time I had chased out the young subject, engaged every single Crooke's Rayo emanator to its maximum setting and aimed them all at the center of the room. There I took refuge. There I thought. There, but for a brief foray to retrieve stationary, I have remained to this moment. When the clarity came to me, it was as the lifting of a heavy velvet curtain at the theatre, when from darkness a wondrous tableau was suddenly and magically made evident. I was, and still remain, overwhelmed by the joy of what my mind is now able to comprehend without the throbbing tentacles pulsing and choking its workings.

I am bewildered at how, in that small moment of insanity that gripped me, I was compelled to lay waste to my beloved machine. For there it lay a few yards off toppled to the ground in hundreds of pieces. Mister Tesla would now never know what had grown from the idea he had planted in me all those years ago. Perhaps this letter would be enough, but of the machine and its ten year journey to creation, nothing survives.

At least I know that for a few moments, I have lived life as a free man. Moreover, I have saved the life of one Prosper-René Blondlot, who will somehow find his way to completing this study and discover the nature of succubus, perhaps freeing us all from their grips. I cannot imagine to what heights the human race might alight when this burden and dreadfulness has been shaken from the world. If I die today contributing to that eventual triumph, I end my days a happy man, for in any case no human being could ever know such hideous truths lurk upon their own selves and long live.

I can write no longer as my eyesight is now failing completely and I feel a dryness throughout my head. A hard pounding in my chest. I have taken a relaxing tonic meant to spur sleep, and it too is now working upon me.

Thank you Abigail for all your kindnesses to me. I regret that this note may bring you some distress, but know that with knowledge comes power. These horrors that suck and cling to us are now found out, and their end shall not be long coming. Toward that inevitable moment, please see that this note finds its way, in some manner, to Mr. Tesla, with my kindest regards, for if he joins with Blondlot, they are certain to succeed.

As for me, all is lost, but peacefully so. Somehow, somewhere, however, I hear, or rather I sense, a peculiar joy. A mirth. It is not a pleasant feeling and I do not understand what it means. But I go to it freely.

M.

There the manuscript ends.

What actually became of Morris Stanley I have not been able to discover. No conflicting records exist, so it is possible that he died as he wished that fateful night. Nor am I certain if any of this information was ever relayed to Nikolai Tesla as he requested of my great Aunt (who, as far as I know, had no connection with him whatsoever). If it was, there is no mention of it in Tesla's public papers, and the fact that the original letter is now in my hands makes me think she did nothing but hide it away. Admittedly, there remain countless reams of Tesla documents in sealed government archives, so it is not entirely certain.

What is certain, from a brief survey of the public record, is that Professor Blondlot, despite his earlier scientific renown, was soon afterwards publicly debunked as a fraud for his quixotic quest for elusive N-Rays and theories of bio-radiation. All indications are that he descended into madness and paranoia before being expelled from his post at Universite-Nancy. While he never publicly mentioned the creatures that Stanley claims they saw together, it was said that he was plagued by constant and unending nightmares to the end of his days.

Knowing all this, I cannot help but consider upon reading this letter, if one were credulous enough to take it at face value, that even in his final victory poor Morris found himself deceived. For what was gained by his death except his continued silence and the inevitable madness of Blondlot?

Of course, fascinating as it is to read, it is absurd to give this strange tale any weight beyond that of terminally sick man's final hallucination, so seeking logic behind Stanley's actions is rather pointless. I can only assume that the author of the note was as unstable and delusional as Blondlot soon became, and that excessive exposure to radiation over many years caused some form of psychosis to them both.

I categorically refuse to consider the alternative.

Thy Bloody and Invisible Hand

June 15, 1953.

Three years ago I treated a friend of mine to a beer and then he smashed my skull with a hammer.

While that was just the first of my torments, I obviously survived. It has, however, taken me until now to piece together the bizarre reason for my misfortune, and to collect together the various strands of the story.

It begins, apparently, with a certain Myrna Brokenshire upon her discharge from the army in 1948. A clumsy munitions accident at her reserve base in Texas left about a quarter of her skull shattered to bits, and only a miracle spared her brain from major damage (although some doctors subsequently questioned this diagnosis.) The doctors were able to reconstruct her skull and protect the valuable squishy stuff, but not without the help of a large metal plate and several pins holding it all together. A textbook-perfect success, the physical recovery took only about four months. As it turned out, that was the easy part.

Myrna was a crisp, sharp, steel-eyed girl that had enlisted in the WACs right after high school in the patriotic furor of 1944 and soon found herself operating radio equipment and conversing with counterparts halfway around the world. She had no interest in munitions, only in a certain munitions officer, which led her to be in the wrong place at the wrong time in a wrongly distracting manner. Major Dan Tyler, who did not survive the messy detonation, would always haunt Myrna as the one that maybe, possibly, was the real deal, but she would never know for sure, and sorrow was not in her nature.

A difficult year, and a psychiatric examination later, she found herself living in a borrowed trailer in Nevada. She reached out to Carnie Bragg, a childhood friend she had grown up with in California. Carnie had the unfortunate nickname Psycho, as he had studied psychiatry for a couple of years before some never entirely clear incident caused him to drop out. Despite his unfinished education and lack of credentials, Carnie felt himself an expert psychiatrist and caught a greyhound to Ely, Nevada.

Unfortunately for me, I also knew Psycho Bragg. Its possible that I may have also briefly met or somehow overlapped with Myrna, but I don't remember her. For the most part I knew Psycho only from the middle of high school and in college. We were just ordinary guys. I wanted to be a journalist, Psycho wanted to be a psychiatrist or psychologist (I never knew which) like his father. We hung out a lot while at LA Junior College and then he went on to one school and me another, but we stayed in touch.

In retrospect, psychiatry was both the worst possible and yet most obvious choice of careers for Psycho. He had the social skills of a pile of rotting fish and an almost frantically overthinking mind. He analyzed every act and decision to the point of complete catatonia. To say that he had never quite understood love and relationships would be a laughable understatement. Carnie was a loner of storybook proportions, and yet he was convinced that somewhere in this confounding world was an ideal girl just waiting for him to find her. Which explains a good deal of the reason he had little hesitation in traveling all night on a bus when someone he had not spoken to in ten years called out of the blue. She was, after all, a girl. When they were kids they had played together often, and the fact that she was calling made it crystal clear, in his mind at least, that she had missed him ever since. Considering it from this later vantage point, its possible that Myrna was the former "girlfriend" that I had always considered imaginary. He had even shown me a pile of letters, but I figured they were just fakes or from his mom. Maybe I was wrong.

He found Myrna among a collection of trailers just on the outskirts of Ely, which was only a couple of blocks from the center of Ely, a flat, slowly dying town on a desolate stretch of road with the saving grace of having extremely low rents.

"The doctors all say I have schizophrenia" she said. Carnie, being the expert psychiatrist, took very careful notes of the conversation. "They say I have multiple personalities. But that's not what I told them at all. I told them that I have my own desires and thoughts, but that I also have *her* desires and thoughts. She is not me, she is not a part of me or in me or related to me, she just works through me. I think for a while I thought maybe I was schizophrenic myself, but that's not it. I think what I am is some kind of radio."

"A radio."

"Yes. What I have is an ability to hear and feel ghosts. I think it's from the metal plate in my head. Its an antennae."

Here Carnie wrote in his notes that Myrna was "a nutjob." But to his credit he kept that diagnosis to himself and kept taking notes.

"I've come to figure out a lot of things. I've often been conflicted and confused in life, Carnie, and now I know that its because what I want and what the ghosts want are not usually the same thing. But before, before all of it sounded the same in my head, there was a mess of things going on, like when your heart is telling you one thing and your brain is telling you something else and I never knew what to do. Like when your stomach turns in knots when you are near someone you don't even know but want to follow for no good reason. But now, since I've had the plate in my head, its different. It took me a while to figure out what the ringing was, like a dentist drill whining in my head sometimes softly, but after a while I realized that when I was conflicted, some of my desires caused ringing in my head and some didn't. That's when I started becoming aware of the ghosts. When the ghosts want me to do something, I want to do it, but there is a tell, a giveaway in my head that it's not really me wanting it."

"You know, a lot of people are conflicted," said Carnie.

"Yes. I think a lot of people have ghosts. I think maybe everyone has ghosts. It's just that most people can't tell. Most people don't have hunks of metal in their brains."

"Lucky you."

"In a way, I guess. We'll see."

"How about me? Do I have a ghost? Can you see it? Is it my grandma?"

"Okay, well, look, I call them ghosts, because that sort of gets across that they are invisible and not of this world, but its not like they are spirits of dead people. I think they are more like some kind of weird monsters, but I don't like to think of them that way because it's a little creepy. I can't really see them, but I can sort of sense that."

"Sense what?"

"Its sort of disgusting, like a big jellyfish, not like people at all."

"Ghost jellyfish."

"Yes, more or less."

"Right."

"What they look like doesn't matter, it's what they want that matters."

"And what is that?"

"Big picture, I have no idea. Short term, they seem to want to move us around and be near certain people and places. That is why people fall in love. I'm convinced of it now. People are always wondering why this or that person is with this or that utterly wrong person, what makes someone attractive to somebody and not to somebody else, why love ruins everything. Why people throw away their lives to move cross-country with a complete loser. Well it's because of them. I know it. All the stuff we want for irrational reasons is because it's not us wanting it. It's Them. They want us to be with somebody and so we want to also, even if we don't like them, even if we know they are bad for us, we still want to be with them. Makes no sense because it's not us wanting it, but we think it is, so we still do it."

And this is where it starts to get even weirder.

"Yes, by the way, you do have one, a ghost, monster, whatever you want to call it."

"Just one?"

"I think everyone has just one. At least of the people I know and that I can tell."

"So you see it?"

"No. It's not so much seeing it. I sense it in my gut. I feel it in my head. And that's why you are here, because of your ghost." She took a moment to consider her words very carefully, as if concentrating on each one before saying, "A month ago I decided and swore that I would marry you and spend the rest of my life with you if I was given a million dollars."

"A million... where would I get a million dollars? And what makes you think I want to marry you at all? Why don't you give ME a million dollars and maybe I'll think about it. " He laughed a bit, trying to figure out if this really was funny or if she was more crazy than he thought. At the same time though, it proved she was in love with him as he suspected all along.

"I'm not asking you for a million dollars. I'm just saying that IF I get a million dollars, no matter from where, I'll spend my life with you. But if I don't, then I'll never see you again. Period. Ever. The reason I asked you to come here was to prove that I was sincere."

"Well I better be heading off then."

"I'm dead serious. And no, don't go. Spend the night."

The next morning came and she sent Carnie packing back to California. His head swimming with the events of the last 24 hours, he sat in a stupor as the greyhound trudged through the desert. Any doubt he had that this girl was worth a million dollars had been well laid to rest. He called me when he got home and we went out drinking, but he didn't tell me anything about what had happened, only that he wished he were rich and how money made all the difference in the world. He was morbidly depressed and for a while I was worried that he might do something stupid like rob a bank or something. He never stopped talking about money after that.

But days and then weeks went by, and it seemed that Psycho had accepted the fact that his childhood first love had gone off her rocker and that it was probably all for the best that he never see her again. Still, I could see him fall silent and stare off vacantly, as if constantly trying to figure out where and how a fortune in cash could be found for such a lowlife as him.

Then, on a spring afternoon, we were sitting on the steps to his apartment when a creamy yellow Olds 88 pulled up and I saw this woman come out and toward the apartment. Never in a million years would I have guessed that this gorgeous dame was Myrna, but I could feel the air get sucked out of Psycho at the sight of her, and I knew. Maybe somewhere under that hair she had a metal plate, but it made me wish all women did.

"Hi honey. You in the market for a wife?" she said walking up.

Before too long she had told us about Major Dan Tyler and the accident at the army base. What Myrna only a few days ago discovered was that not only was Dan Tyler an only son, he was the only son of a very wealthy, grief-stricken family who eventually realized that their son's mistake had caused a life changing injury to the daughter-in-law that they had hoped to have. An agent for the family found her in Ely and presented her with a gift, or as the Tyler's put it, "an amends and apology" of one million dollars.

"The thing is, honey, that monsters are like anything else. Once you know what they want, you have them beat. If they can make me want me to do things, then I figured they can just as easily make other people want to do things. They did. They delivered, and here I am. Lets go buy a house and live happily ever after."

Now, as long as I live I will never hear an offer a tenth as good as that one, but Psycho seemed to be hyperventilating. He walked backwards away from Myrna and ran into his apartment where he slammed the door and locked himself in. Myrna followed him and tried to coax him out, but he wouldn't answer the door.

"I guess he has to think about it," she said with a smile as she came out, "you know a good hotel in these parts?" I recommended a couple and she asked which was the most expensive and where that one was. Then she turned a bit more pensive. "Look, I know he thought I was crazy before, but just tell him this: there's no magic, there's no evil, there's no spells and hocus pocus, there's only commerce, and you get the best deal you can." She started to walk away, "I'll be at the hotel until I find us a house."

At that point I figured I had to know what was going on, so I went down to the store, bought a six pack, came back to the apartment and, with the offer of free beer and a friendly ear, got Psycho to open the door.

He was glistening with sweat. "I can't believe it. I can't – I won't believe it. It can't be true" he raved over and over. "I love her, I've always loved her, do you understand? Its not some other creature that loves her, its ME. I know it. I won't let it be somebody – or some thing else." While I now know what he was talking about, I did not at the time, nor did I grasp the meaning of the conversation when it turned toward the subject of controlling his own fate.

"If she can do it, I can do it" he kept repeating, pacing the floor. "I know all about the brain, I'm a psychologist, I can figure this out. If there are fucking creatures using me then goddamnit I'm going to..."

"Going to what?" I asked, "What are you talking about?"

He came and went in the room shuffling things around, as if looking for something, "I have to know, but I need to test first, I need to find out where and how to do it, I need... I need..." and then he looked at me. He had a desperate, sad face, and I started to say something. I was focused on his face, trying to calm him down. I didn't see the hammer.

The days and weeks that followed are a blur of horror and pain that I was only barely conscious of. It was six weeks later that the police found me in the streets, bandaged head covered in blood and glass shards stuck in my hands. I do not recall escaping, but it seems I went through a window. At the hospital the surgeons worked for three days trying to repair my skull. There were pieces of metal and needles and pins, wires and even a nail in my brain. They got it all out, but it took almost two years to fully recover. Now I'm mostly fine, though my smile is a bit crooked as a few muscles on the left side of my face don't seem to work anymore.

What the police found when they went to Psycho's house was worse. I was not the only experiment. Two other people were in the apartment, tied up, heads covered in metal probes and blood soaked bandages. One was dead. The other survived much like me.

They also found Psycho. He must have reached a point in his experiments where he found what he was looking for, because if he wanted to hear the creatures like Myrna, there was only one way. He will probably never speak or walk again. If he can hear or see the ghost monsters, I hope it is sufficient solace, for all that remains of him is an incapacitated, drooling body barely able to breathe on its own, and a misshapen head with six metal posts fired in with a newly purchased pneumatic hammer that the doctors were too afraid to remove.

Myrna lives in Pacific Palisades overlooking the ocean with a new husband and a baby on the way. She has thus far kept her end of the peculiar "bargain" and visits Psycho in the nursing home once a week, although I suspect she has not told her new husband the whole story about her commerce with monsters.

Among the Unbelonged

Helena

A bus. Possibly the least dramatic of places. Where endless hours of monotonous rumbling and hypnotic shadows numb the brain into a stupor, here our story comes to its conclusion. One way or the other, there will be an outcome. Somebody is delusional, and somebody is sane, and the next twenty-four or so hours will decide which is which. So with nothing but the drone of the tires to distract me, this is probably as good a time as any to put down an account of what brought me here. If anyone makes a movie of this, I'll probably be in a Ferrari, or a speedboat, or something else really extraordinary, and this final chase to the end of the world would happen at something more than forty-five miles per hour. But that's not reality. Reality is usually really slow. At least for me.

I am an English teacher. I've come to accept that this is what the vast majority of people on the planet will recall of me long after they have ceased to remember my name, if they ever bothered to know it at all. Its Tyson, by the way, my name, but thousands of teenagers will only remember Mr. Welles, or, more likely, that boring English teacher. I once thought of myself as a writer who taught English, but the passing of the years has made this charade less and less believable.

This is only important insofar as the teaching of high school English allows for the periodic hallucinogenic overlap between the written and real Romeos and Juliets, and the discomforting realization that humanity lacks a page in its instruction manual when it comes to romance and attraction. For what causes good Romeo to be in love with fair Juliet? To disregard family, fortune and even life for the sake of being physically near this one person? On this essential point, on this crux of the crux of all matters romance, even the inventor of romance, Shakespeare himself, is completely silent. Love, as it occurs between these two star crossed characters, happens between a glance and a breath and four days later there are five dead bodies. It makes no sense at all. That Shakespeare clearly refuses to even try to make sense of it seems to be the point he is trying to make. This thing just happens, for no reason at all, and then there is blood and violence and passion and wrath and everything changes for everybody because of something that does not even warrant a single line in the play. Once Romeo asks

> "What lady is that, which doth
> enrich the hand
> Of yonder knight?"

it is already a done deed, he is stricken, and enamored, which he confesses immediately. He is in love before even knowing her name. Having completely forgotten his prior love Rosaline in the single beat of a heart.

Why Juliet? There are hundreds of other girls at the ball. If she is the fairest, then why are all the others in the room not equally enchanted and bewitched? Impossible to know. It just IS. The way it all plays out is the work of puppetmaster gods and spirits and the best thing you can do is stay clear til the carnage ends. Standing year after year in front of crowds of hormonally unbalanced teenagers and trying to make sense of it made me feel that I understood nothing about either literature or life itself.

Until now. Now I have the missing page of instructions, which makes it all crystal clear. Or, equally plausibly, I have a head full of lies and insanity. We shall see soon enough, although neither outcome is without its horrors.

My part in what is actually going on here is, admittedly, tangential at best. My only real significance is that I have been uniquely positioned to offer this account, which is likely to be the only one of its kind. I came upon the main players by accident, much as Romeo came upon Juliet. He did not go to that ball with the intention of laying waste to his life and four others. I did not wander into Pilgrim Books that afternoon, now eighteen months ago, with the thought that it would lead to a global cataclysm, and yet both he and I found that our intentions often have little to do with our course.

Her name was Helena, and she worked at this peculiar little bookshop filled with art prints, handmade pamphlets, underground zines, herbs and a multitude of tiny artisanal items tinged with a vague sorcery. What was it about her? Everything and nothing. I point you to Juliet. And to Lisa, my now inexplicable wife, from whom I have been separated for five years. There is no human explanation that does anything beyond describe the symptoms of it having already happened. For me, it was the nauseating tightening of the stomach and inability to look Helena in the eyes. I don't remember if it was the same with Lisa. Like Rosaline, she was just what came before.

Through a steady stream of visits to the shop, where I usually bought some odd wall hanging made of mystic twigs from some remote Honduran village that I still have in its bag, or a xeroxed neo-catholic text on the transformative powers of sexual bondage which remains, predictably, unread, I learned quite a bit about Helena and the vast wonder of her world. Her world involved an inordinate use of the word Beautiful, and she referred to her endless stream of friends, male and female, as Beloved or Lover. When she smelled something nice, I would see her visibly swoon and sway. She would tell me about the smells and echoes in the little Catholic church she attended, about meditating in an oak tree during a thunderstorm, about how she was writing poems with ink she made herself, about metempsychosis and how she thought in a previous life she had been Gallic, because she would sometimes dream in French. She was as different from me and my little sensible life as it would be possible to get. I usually added little to our "conversations" – actually more of a series of monologues that I would prompt with some innocent question. Sometimes I would be able to interject a literary reference to something she was saying, but it was usually little more than "Ah, yes, just like Puck in Midsummer Nights Dream" or something equally witless. After all the weeks of getting to know her karmic universe I came to realize that somewhere in all that wide-eyed joy and mystery she hid a little corner of sadness and fear that I did not completely grasp until a few months later.

It would be amusing but ultimately pointless to recount the number of times and ways in those six months that I fruitlessly toiled to attract Helena's attention. Suffice to say that the results were comically inept. It was at around the six month mark, when my delirium had convinced me that, as a writer, I could create a book of poetry dedicated to her and slip it inadvertently into her store shelves that I realized it had to stop, that I had gone over the edge. It was clear that I would not be able to do anything to make her notice me. It was hopeless. She talked and confided in me as a customer, or as a bartender would chat with a regular, but she rarely asked questions about me or cared if I left, or seemed particularly pleased to see me. Not that she was *dis*pleased to see me, just that her reaction to me entering the store was the same calm joy she offered every person that wandered in.

This moment of decision came to me as I sat at the café a half block or so from Pilgrim Books, in the middle of writing one of the now aborted poems. I had started having coffee there several times a week in order to occasionally bump into the object of my desires. As it happened, she was there at the time, and sitting as usual with this lanky man. Ah, yes. The Lanky Man. Right then, mere seconds after the decision that I would cease my fruitless romantic quest, when I looked over to her table, that was when I first became faintly aware that there were things in the world that I did not see, or to be more exact, did not perceive at all. This lanky person had in fact been hanging around the edges of Helena since I first saw her. He was in the store that first day I went in it. He had been with her at this coffee shop a dozen times. But only now, today, had his existence actually coalesced in my brain. There was someone with her. I had been blind to this the entire time.

"Hey," I said, walking past in a labored "casual" manner.

She glanced up with her serene face. "Hey."

I extended my hand to her friend. "I'm Tyson."

"I know. I'm Thantos."

"You know?" I said, my chest contracting in excitement. Perhaps Helena had been mentioning me, and my attempts to stand out had not been so laughable after all? Maybe this wasn't her boyfriend or lover, but just an acquaintance or co-worker.

"Yes, we've met," said Thantos, and then a little ruefully added, "A couple of times."

"Thantos is my brother," Helena said softly, "Remember?" It was a strange tone, almost a faint pleading that I had somehow stepped in something and needed to walk it back.

"Oh. I'm sorry, I-"

"Its okay."

"No no, of course, I remember."

I felt, well, I didn't *feel* terrible, but felt like I somehow was terrible without feeling it. Because really I did not remember him at all.

Helena was up and gathering her things. "I have to get back to the shop. You guys go ahead and chat, or whatever guys do, punch each other and spit and stuff."

It was a little awkward but I thought I might as well spend a minute with her brother, but I swear as I watched her leave he entirely slipped my mind and I started to walk off.

"Well, bye then," he said, and it completely startled me. I had forgotten all about him. But I had not forgotten the odd plea in Helena's tone, the one that gently asked me to be friendly to her brother. So I mumbled and stumbled a bit and sat down and we began to talk.

Thantos

I studied his face seriously while sitting there. I wanted to be sure I remembered the next time what he looked like, so I would not appear a fool in front of his sister.

"I know what you are doing." He said.

"What? What do you mean?"

"Don't worry about it. It happens to everyone. I'm invisible. Have been for years. Don't sweat it. Its not your fault."

I tried to laugh it off, but he was serious. He said he had been invisible to people since high school, and he had the idea that it was some kind of "Quantum Field" or some such. Once he got to talking, he just went on for a long spell, talking about the vast gulf between what people perceived and what was real, what he could see and others couldn't, about how fundamental science is being suppressed by a grand conspiracy, how the Vulcans understood everything better. I sensed that he didn't have many opportunities to do this and he was trying to fit a lot of talking in before I got tired of him, which actually happened quite quickly, but I continued to listen, because he said his sister worried about his invisibility.

"She's afraid she's going to stop seeing me, too. I can see her doing the same thing you were doing before, studying my face, trying to memorize it. When I catch her doing it, I try and pretend like I didn't notice, but she knows I do. She gets so sad I can't bear it. It makes me think that maybe its fine that it's all probably ending soon."

Uh, what?

"What do you mean?" I asked, trying to sound casual and not at all concerned.

He looked at me thoughtfully, "Nothing. I'm thinking maybe I'll move away is all. Maybe, I don't know, back to California."

But I knew that wasn't what he meant at all. Thantos had some serious mental health issues going on, I felt for sure that he had accidently let something slip he had not intended.

There is a certain special kind of shame that one has when you know your motives are not somehow right, humane, nor even really human. I felt this almost immediately when leaving Thantos that afternoon. I knew, without a doubt, that he was clinically depressed and possibly suicidal. Moreover, I knew he was an entirely pleasant, intelligent, and seemingly kind individual who deserved better and really *really* needed a friend to talk to. But I knew that the only reason I cared, and the only reason I would be helping him, or even talking to him at all, was to further my relationship with his sister. It was so base, so crass, that I cringe from even admitting it now. I really did not care if Thantos lived or died so long as whatever happened earned me respect and brownie points from his sister. For Juliet, there is no price too high, even Romeo's humanity. How was that possible for someone who thought himself an enlightened, charitable person?

Nevertheless, whatever my motivations, I did end up taking a modest interest in Thantos and becoming something of a friend, as much as that was possible with someone who was prone to hallucination and borderline sociopathic, albeit a resigned form of sociopath to be sure. I came to understand his lunacy to a fine degree, learning to let him ramble in pseudoscience jargon for a while about conspiracies and obstructions to truth, then gently moving the topic to something more prosaic that we could both discuss rationally and amicably, like TV shows or the stupidity of Texas politicians.

We did not discuss one thing that, reluctantly, we grew to agree on. He was, in fact, nearly invisible. When we would order coffee, the barista would only talk to me, even if Thantos was clearly in front of me, a waitress would bring one water or one set of silverware to a table we were sharing and be invariably surprised to find another person there, panhandlers and street charlatans would push him out of the way to get to me as if he was an empty shopping cart. One might assume that he was grotesque, deformed or dressed like a lecherous hobo, but nothing could be further from the truth. He was tall, handsome in a gawky sort of way, with his hair combed and his shirts clean. He looked like your basic accountant, civil servant, or middle management type. I could flatter myself that it was because of my own overpowering charisma and physique that he was rendered so inconsequential, but I do own a mirror and considered myself, at least at the time, among the non-delusional.

The cause of this invisibility therefore became a nagging puzzle that annoyed me each time I thought of Thantos; and when I grew to accept it wasn't simply a paranoia of his, I started doing some research, joining chat rooms, sending queries in more and more obscure corners of the web. One night, after again turning up nothing, I amused myself by clicking on a link to photos of "invisible people" which were the usual collection of semi-clever images and captions that clog the internet like sisyphean snowdrifts. Except that one of them drew my eye. It was a snarkily captioned photo of a flyer posted on a bulletin board in some university hallway.

ARE YOU AN INVISIBLE ALIEN FROM ANOTHER WORLD?

It went on, in a couple of short paragraphs, to precisely and concisely describe my new friend Thantos. Exactly. The person who shot and posted the picture obviously thought it was hilarious, or a joke, but I recognized the same call for help that I got from Helena and Thantos. A nervous fear of exclusion and of inexorably vanishing into nothingness.

There was contact information at the bottom of the flyer. A blog/website for a group calling itself The Clarity Gathering. Conveniently enough, the group was based just a couple of hundred miles away in north Texas, near Wichita Falls, and posted a bi-weekly meet and greet for "anyone who felt they belonged among the unbelonged."

After Helena and Thantos expressed an interest in this group, it should come as no surprise that a good deal of my mind became preoccupied with the fantasy of being on an extended road trip with Helena, wondering what we would talk about, what she would wear, the possibilities of an overnight stay in some little motel where who knew what could happen. But this elaborate construct disintegrated when she came down with the flu and had to beg off, but insisted -damn her to hell- that the two of us go anyway without her. So we drove off, just me and whats-his-name, Thantos.

These invisibles gathered in the meeting hall of small church, which in Texas is often the only public meeting space available for folks with no money. I don't know what I expected, really, but I was braced for the worst: a dysfunctional crowd of crazy rural bumpkins spouting conspiracy theories that we would nod at for a few minutes and then quietly try to make some excuse to get some fresh air and make a break for the car. I was therefore a bit disappointed, to tell the truth, when we were greeted by about a dozen very calm, well dressed people sitting facing a whiteboard filled with either calculus equations or Martian (which are, as far as I can ascertain, indistinguishable).

"Come in, come in," said the woman standing at the whiteboard, "Are you here for Clarity?" At that moment, for the first time, my ears pricked up at the weird cult sound of that phrase. Nonetheless, we said yes, came in and sat down in the back.

"Excellent! I am Dr. Strauss, welcome to the group. Which of you is the one that's really here, you can't both be really here."

"It's me" said Thantos, "My name is Thantos Panagos."

"Good to meet you, Thantos, and why are you here?"

Thantos hesitated a moment, a short moment, and glanced around the room as if trying to quickly size up what it would be safe to say. Some variation of "I feel invisible" or "I suffer from Depersonalization Disorder" or something like that, weighed against the more agnostic "I'm not sure." The last thing I expected was "Nobody but me can see that the world may soon to be destroyed."

I wanted to become invisible myself at that point, but the small group seemed completely unfazed. "That's intriguing," said Dr. Strauss, "Now I want to ask you a couple of very important questions."

"I don't think I'm crazy" said Thantos.

"That's not really important," replied Strauss, "what is important is if you have ever had cancer."

What the--?

"Uh...Yes. When I was little. It was pretty serious."

"Cancer usually is. Now, the second question is even more important. Does the term Radivex mean anything to you?"

"Of course, that was the treatment. I came…" and Thantos paused again, something clicking in his mind. But the whole rest of the room was suddenly very agitated and worried, whispering back and forth, even Strauss seemed suddenly more unnerved. "I would come with my mother to Wichita Falls," continued Thantos, "to the clinic, it was really close to here."

"Yes, it was. You were cured it seems."

"Completely."

Strauss addressed the others. "We have a new member, it seems…" she held up her hand to quiet some of them down, "And before we have him explain why he thinks the world is doomed, we should explain to him why he is here." The room quieted down, but was still noticeably more nervous.

Thantos was looking as puzzled as I was. "You think the cancer made me this way?"

"No," said Strauss, "Nor do any of us actually believe we are invisible Vulcans, although that was a working theory for many of us for a while. We have come to believe it was the cure that made you, and us, this way. Everyone here was a Radivex patient. Every one of us had virtually zero chance of survival. Radivex cured us all. As a matter of fact, Radivex had a 100%

success rate. It was, and remains, the most effective cancer cure ever, period."

"So, what's that got to do with me, or us? Why doesn't every cancer patient see things like I do?"

"Ah, indeed, why not? That's the big mystery. Radivex was an experimental radiation treatment, a clinical trial. A very limited trial restricted to a small number of terminal patients. The thing that we discovered, together, over the last couple of years as our group formed, is that after that initial clinical trial of some 42 patients, all of which recovered completely, with no physical side effects, the Radivex technology was never used again. Never mentioned again. It just disappeared as if it never existed. The clinic where the trials took place is now a vacant field, the doctors who performed it, and the engineers who built the apparatus have also, it seems, vanished into obscurity, as has all research and reference to Radivex in any medical journal. So there are only about a couple of dozen people still alive that had the treatment, some of them were already quite old when they got it and have passed away in the intervening years from other causes. Half of that number is right here, people who lived within a few hundred miles of the clinic or relocated here for the treatment and never left. As far as we can tell, every single person so far that had Radivex suffers from The Clarity."

"We aren't the first," said a small, pale little man. "I'm Robert, and I found the writings of Antonelli d'Siena. There's a link on the group site."

"Well," said Strauss, "we don't know for sure he's talking about the same thing, but it's eerily similar, from a 15th century perspective anyway. But more importantly, what can you tell us about the end of the world, Mr. Panagos?"

"Well," said Thantos, "It's probably best if I show you." So he took out his laptop and punched up some animated video clip of a bunch of white dots. "These are asteroids. I'm an astrophysicist, until recently employed, until I tried to show people this. Look at these two asteroids here. I'm going to play a 90-day timelapse, and tell me what you see." He pressed play and we stared at dots that twinkled and drifted for about ten seconds. I was fairly certain that Thantos was never an astrophysicist, and that this was just some random footage he downloaded from some conspiracy site on the internet, but I was not his target audience. His new clarity co-horts were eagerly lapping it up.

Two people who hadn't spoken before, a big hairy guy and a little asian woman both said "Helix" after just a few seconds. Thantos looked stunned, "You saw it?"

"That's what I saw too, I think, if helix means a sort of spirally thing," chimed Pale Robert.

The others all nodded and agreed in various mumbles that they had seen the two dots spiraling around each other. They played the clip several times. I stared at those damn dots for all I was worth and I will swear to this day that they never budged or moved at all. But I was the only one there that didn't see them "helix" across the screen.

"So what does that mean?" asked Pale Robert.

"What you are seeing" replied Thantos, "are two small bodies that are obviously orbiting a larger dark body as it moves through space. This large dark body is not visible, but the smaller asteroids orbiting it are. My calculations are what make this alarming. Whatever is in the center is enormous, and its going to impact the earth in 8 months. Any college undergrad in astronomy would be able to see this and figure out its trajectory, it really isn't very difficult. But everyone said I was hallucinating, that I was having another of my "episodes" where things were not as they seemed. I've shown this video to hundreds of people, but until tonight nobody has ever seen the asteroids even move at all. My guess was that something about them was out of phase with normal A-Phase people. I call them the B-Phase asteroids."

The group swallowed up Thantos. I have to admit they weren't unlikeable. The name they chose was, beyond the new age-y sound of it, a reference to the local ghost town, Clara.

Some of them apparently recalled visiting the spooky abandoned old streets and ramshackle cemetery when they were coming for treatments, and now they themselves had become ghosts in the world. But there was a creepy cult factor too. The group did not just see themselves as victims, they saw themselves as Chosen, with a capital C. When they spoke of clarity, it was Clarity, of being able to see things that regular people could not. Their patron saint, this Antonelli, wrote of being able to see reality for the first time:

> True enlightenment comes with the vanquishing
> of the hundred-limbed demons of darkness that
> forever endeavor to cloud our minds and
> obfuscate the truths both great and minute. They
> toil for the great Leviathan, their spectral mother,
> against all human minds. To what end they
> shackle our thoughts we can have no doubt, that it
> is to keep us from illumination.

Apparently Antonelli had built, or forged, an enormous "bell" from an ore he called the metal of St. Peter's shield, a glowing metal twice as heavy as lead, and when inside this bell, he was able to think clearly and escape the demons that tried to mislead and confuse him.

In the solitude of the bell, which should be wholly dark but instead has a serene luminance, as perhaps the metal had never fully cooled, and held a reminder of the forge deep inside, here I can comprehend the world as God intended, but failing to write my thoughts down renders them phantoms at the very moment I emerge from its sanctuary. The light of day holds the darkness of the demons, of confusion and wickedness. In the light, I am blind.

These writings, alas, were Antonelli's undoing, for they proved him a heretic, a traitor and either a madman or sorcerer, for which he was summarily hanged. The members of the group had already come up with a theory that this bell was made of some kind of Uranium/Radium ore that mimicked the effects of the radiation treatment they had received. They had also adopted as the seal of the group a drawing by their martyr Antonelli of an evil octopus-like demon being slain by St. Alexander with the caption "tenebris victis," Interestingly, St. Alexander, the patron saint of philosophers, had similarly found the light of truth only deep inside the impenetrable darkness of a coal mine.

Darkness Vanquished

What did all this nonsense from these self-obsessed lunatics mean? It was all very interesting, and hearing them talk would convince anyone that they had done a lot of research and knew their shit. But I teach literature, and I've read *Foucault's Pendulum*, and I deal with teenagers, so I know what a hermetic argument sounds like. Thantos, however, did not. And to be fair, these seemed to be people he connected with in a way I knew he did not normally connect with anyone.

He wanted to know more, to discuss things well past the time the church custodian wanted them out of the building. He decided to stay in Wichita Falls for the weekend, then the week, then I stopped hearing from him at all. Which was a great development, because then I could be worried enough to go see Helena.

In the intervening week, however, I kept wracking my brain trying to figure out what it was about the rantings of Antonelli that seemed familiar. I had certainly never heard of him before, and it was the kind of singular nightmare prose that was unlikely to be copied elsewhere. I spent the week re-reading Lovecraft, thinking that maybe I was recalling some story involving Cthulu, but that wasn't it. As it happened, it was also now the dead of winter in Texas, which kicks summer – our only other season - away in the blink of an eye, and I began to daydream about a trip south to Mexico. It seemed to be completely unrelated, I know, but every time I was trying to find whatever was bugging me, I wound up thinking about cold, dark places with squiggly slimey monsters and wishing I could think about something else, warmer, nicer, monsterless. Soon I was daydreaming about Mexico. I started forming a picture in my head of the warmth, the margaritas, the lack of students and grading, the lack of Thantos. Mexico. Jalisco, to be exact. Oh to be in Jalisco.

Jalisco? Really? What the heck was in Jalisco? *Where* the heck was Jalisco? It didn't really matter, I guess, it sounded Mexican, and spicy.

I did not at that point know about Duncan Grimsley, but it's a good time to mention him, because if I had, it would have bugged me. I don't like coincidences. I read a lot of lousy fiction written by 10th graders, and ninety percent of their plots would go nowhere except for the standard series of miraculous coincidences. So if I had known that one of the guys from the cult of clarity was at that moment in the eastern desert of Jalisco doing some very odd excavations, I would have stopped right then and questioned what had led me to think about Mexico to begin with. But I didn't, so I set in motion that afternoon the events that led me to this bus right now.

Helena, on the other end of the spectrum from me, not only loves coincidences but counts on them. She assumes the interconnections and the hand of god, or gods, are in every movement and decision. "I'm just part of the team, we all are," she says, so when we talked that afternoon about Thantos, and she said, out of the blue, "We should all take a trip to Mexico together" it did not strike her as at all strange that I had been thinking of going there just that that morning. To her it was the opposite: proof of the validity of the sentiment. Synchronicity was evidence that emotions were true, that choices were enlightened and inevitable, that randomness was not at work but rather some deeper understanding was being shared. I'm afraid that my surprise served the purpose of validating and cementing in her mind that a southern voyage was not just desirable and fun, but a now sacred necessity, a beckoning that we both heard and had to be followed.

Unfortunately for us both, the weirdness of the moment was not able to overcome my infatuation's response, which was an adrenaline rush that knocked my head sideways. We had, finally, formed some kind of bond, Helena and I, which began with Thantos and was now sealed by our upcoming spiritual quest. From that moment on, we talked not about what I would do and what she would do but what *We* would do. We would solve the riddle of Thantos by going away on this trek, and find ourselves, find Thantos, and return renewed.

It was giddy stuff. She opened up to me about her brother, and how, just as he suspected, she had to force herself to remember him. She felt connected to everyone, as if by a cord in her heart, except for the one person she felt she should hold most dear, and that was beloved Thantos, who was almost a stranger to her each time she saw him. She pulled out a pile of pictures and scrapbooks she had with her at the store. "I page through his things every day to keep him in my thoughts, his pictures, writings, letters, awards, all the things that prove he is real." I watched her first with the warmth of seeing a saint at work, but it slowly turned to growing alarm. And for a moment, it was if I had been slapped in the face. She was paging through all these Thantos mementos, which included citations from MIT and CalTech, his credentials at JPL, his invitation to join a team at CERN. A photograph of him with Stephen fucking Hawking. I just froze.

Incredibly, Thantos was not insane. He was not a charlatan and a lunatic. He was exactly what he claimed to be: an astrophysicist with impeccable credentials and jaw droppingly brilliant beyond measure. Which meant, of course, that we were probably all completely screwed beyond belief.

Duncan

When we finally got back together with Thantos a few days later, I saw him through an entirely different set of eyes. He and his new friends had concocted an experiment to test a hypothesis. A couple of them had connections at UT Austin and had arranged to run the test there. This Thantos, in charge of a scientific study, was not the timid Thantos of the coffee shop, afraid he was vanishing. He was meticulously prepared, efficient and exacting. A man completely in his element. The test itself appeared to be quite lame, if truth be told. It went like this: a diverse group of people were shown some short videos and asked to describe them. First there were a series of random sequences of dots moving and not moving across a yellow background, and people were asked if some circled dots moved and how. Then it was followed by an animated version of the two "helixing" dots. Subjects were asked a few simple questions about the animation. Then it was replaced by the actual footage of fuzzy white dots against a black background, and the questions were asked again. Finally, there was a one minute explanation of what the video actually was, specifically "footage of asteroids in space near earth", and then the subjects were shown and quizzed about the footage again.

I thought this experiment was ridiculously stupid, because either you see something or you don't. The results proved otherwise. Every single subject, save one, stated that they saw the two dots moving across the screen in a wavy pattern during the first two screenings, but claimed the picture was static or difficult to know for sure on the third viewing. It didn't make any sense.

I can safely say that I was transformed that night, because it was clear that I could no longer trust my own mind. I watched as subjects claimed to see things move one minute and then completely forget they had, or claim they were confused. The conclusion seemed impossible but unavoidable: as soon as people realized that the dots were asteroids and not just animated dots, their minds refused to see them move, and even erased the memory of them having previously moved. So did that mean that I couldn't trust my own eyes regarding the dots? Were they really moving? I had no way to test the theory, since I could not forget that they were asteroids, but what possible difference could it make? How many other things was my mind capable of blocking out or hiding from me? If it can hide asteroids, why not other things, or people? Like Thantos. Like the invisibles. Ah, yes, the dots may not move for me, but they do connect.

There was one subject in the experiments that was the exception. He saw the dots move both before and after the explanation. Which was the second part of the experiment, because this was one of the invisibles that had not been in Wichita Falls the first night and knew nothing of the asteroids. He, like all the invisibles, saw the dots move every time. This was Duncan Grimsley.

Duncan had only in the last year been contacted by the Clarity gang and this was his first face to face meeting with the other invisibles. He was particularly excited as he saw the results of the experiment because it confirmed that he himself had not been hallucinating for the past ten years regarding his own quixotic quest. "I was pretty damn sure I was a nutjob. There's no way you can see stuff nobody sees for ten years and not doubt your heads right."

"So Thantos here sees asteroids that move, and I think we've pretty much proven that they move today," said Dr. Strauss, "What is it you think you see?"

Duncan hesitated a bit, with the uncertain caution of someone who has been mocked far too many times, "Well, you know, its complicated and, you see, I'm a geologist, you know, and a sort of amateur palentologist, and well, " he began haltingly until Pale Robert cut him off.

"Cut to the chase, we're all nutjobs, we'll believe anything."

Duncan shrugged and said "I see a giant underground whale."

For the last decade it seems, Duncan had been crisscrossing the desert in central Mexico taking various seismic and magnetic readings, almost entirely by himself. He was convinced that somewhere deep under the ground, miles under the ground, were the remains of a gigantic creature unlike anything else ever seen on earth.

"Well you know, first, I'm not all sure it's a physical skeleton," he said a few hours later when he had gathered his research items, "I'm just saying that it sorta kinda makes the image of one. But y'all be the judge." He punched up a series of surveys maps with thousands of dots on them, all overlaid on top of each other. It definitely looked like a bunch of dots. "Now wait a minute, lemme show you when its pulled into the 3D program." And a few moments later the thousands of dots resolved into a large 3D blob of dots spinning in space. He looked at us. I looked around at the others. In an eerie repetition of that night in Wichita Falls, they were wide-eyed and excited like little schoolgirls. Unlike that night, however, I understood that my eyes don't show me everything, so I nudged Thantos and asked what he saw.

"Its just the biggest damn whale in the history of whales is all."

If the invisibles are to be believed, and at this point I had just started to assume they were all smarter than I was, this "whale" was literally over a thousand miles from end to end. It wasn't "precisely" a whale, according them, it didn't exactly correspond anatomically, it didn't seem to have a mouth or appendages, but in terms of its overall shape it was either "whale" or "whale-shaped thing" so they just went with "whale."

"And this is underground?" asked Thantos.

"Yes sir. Near as I can figure it's a thousand kilometers down."

"A *thousand* kilometers?"

"Yessir."

"That's in the mantle, that's impossible."

"Yessir. It is. If you're talking something solid."

The big hairy guy, whose name I will never remember, chimed in, "This is an electromagnetic skeleton. It's a phantom whale."

"That's near as I reckon, too. You can see why I wasn't keen on saying so. Sounds a ways off the norm, talking about 2000 kilometer ghost whale buried a thousand kilometers underground, and as most folks don't even see the shape at all I figured I was on a one-way express to the funny house til you guys."

Again, I did not see the evidence, but I thought I did see the pattern. "It's a B-Phase Whale."

"Not anymore" said Dr. Strauss.

"What do you mean?"

"It seems clear now that the asteroids themselves are not invisible, so long as people are not aware they are looking at asteroids. My guess is that Duncan here also prefaced his showing of the data with some kind of introduction. If subjects were shown the 3D model as, say, an art project, I would wager they would see the whale. This proves something we have always vaguely known about our condition, about why we call it Clarity, its that regular people have some kind of cognative filter that blocks some things from being seen, and we seem to have lost that."

The next few days while at school I kept thinking that I was suddenly immersed in something as strange as anything in an old issue of *Weird Tales*. And then, as I recalled that someone had said "Phantom Whale" the word phantom connected, and I remembered where I had read that Antonelli stuff before. The high school library contained several volumes of anthologies from science fiction monthlies like *Analog* and *Astounding Stories*, and there I found it.

Science Fact and Fiction Quarterly published what claimed to be a letter written around 1900 by a scientist named Morris Stanley. Stanley claimed in this letter to have made a machine that could see otherwise invisible "tendrilled demons" attached like parasites to all kinds of people, including himself. These demons fed on and warped his thoughts. Furthermore, he discovered that beams of radiation could chase them off, at least temporarily. This was far too close to the mark to be coincidence. Either this author had come across Antonelli's incredibly obscure notebook, or he was describing the same thing independently: something octopuslike, invisible to the eye, that could occlude a mind. But the most valuable bit of information was that he had made a machine that let you see them.

Ekbom's Syndrome

My remarks about this old story drew polite nods from the invisibles until I mentioned offhand the disgraced French scientist Blondlot, who played a supporting role in the tale. Apparently this professor had been the subject of much debate among the group a year or so before, and the connection to him lit up the room like a crack of lightning. They tore through the alleged "letter" in minutes and were soon chattering like possessed typewriters about it. It wasn't even fifteen minutes before Dr. Strauss scrawled "Research Plan" on the whiteboard and I excused myself from the din.The invisibles seemed alarmingly eager to embrace as true a variation of what is called Ekbom's Syndrome. This is psychotic delusion of being infested by parasites. In the case of Stanley's letter, he talks about one giant parasite rather than scores of tiny ones, but aside from scale of the critter, the symptoms seem textbook, and are often linked to paranoia of being controlled.

On the other hand, it illustrates something I grew to realize about the invisibles as a group. They are all unquestionably brilliant, some of the smartest people I've ever seen in a room. But they all seem to have a narrow scope of knowledge and endeavor, in that every one of them is dedicated voraciously to a very hard science. Not difficult hard, I mean one of those that don't allow a lot of interpretation. Math, Physics, Molecular Biology, Geology, Chemistry, Computers, Engineering. Not a single one of them dabbled in anything remotely interpretive or creative. No musicians, painters, journalists or writers, Nothing also that dealt with the human condition, no historians, psychologists, linguists, architects, lawyers. It was all about math, formulas, rigorous proofs. Even the one sort of outlier, William the Fat, who dealt in finance, was essentially a mathematician and computer programmer. He cared nothing about actual companies, products or innovations. He saw an enormous cloud of numbers and probabilities and created algorithms to have those numbers yield money. Radical amounts of money on short notice, it turns out.

When I next came upon Thantos, about two weeks later at Pilgrim Books, he was excited to show me and Helena what he and his new friends called "The Lab." The two of us thought this was rather cute. These overgrown science nerds needed some sort of garage workshop to tinker in, and we figured they would be up to all sorts of Mentos geysers and hovercars. We could not have ever, in a lifetime of guessing, have thought they would have acquired a 10,000 square foot laboratory with every imaginable scientific apparatus, including a wide array of sophisticated medical research equipment. It wasn't until we were well inside and stunned with amazement that we saw the actual horror the lab was for.

"Thantos," whispered Helena with an urgent tone, "who are they?" She was staring at a section of the lab where there were twenty small cages, similar to jail cells or oversized kennel cells. Each 6-foot cube held a person. I could see that two of them were just children. All of them were either sleeping or possibly sedated.

"Experiments," he said calmly, "we're looking for Tyson's parasites. Don't worry, they all volunteered."

"Even the children?"

"I think Julia borrowed them from her sister." I don't know how Thantos could have so lacked any knowledge of how his sister would react to this. But she began to weep even before we came upon Pale Robert and one of the "experiments." I had to take her outside immediately.

She clung to me outside in the parking lot for half an hour. It was appalling and incredible what was going on inside. She was inconsolable. I was in heaven.

"That last man..." she said at last, "he was dead."

"Now, come on, you don't know that"

"I do. He was dead. I could feel his absence when I saw him."

"I admit he didn't look too good. But..."

"They are killing people for experiments. They are killing their own families and friends... oh God..." she broke down into sobs again, "Thantos asked me last night if I wanted to help him with an experiment... I thought he meant, you know, something normal."

She broke down again into tears, unable to believe that her brother would have put her in one of those kennels if she had "volunteered". Finally, she said, "I have to get him out of here. Away from those people. Wait here." And she went back into the lab.

A few moments later she came back out. Distraught. Thantos-less. She could barely look at me as she went into the car. "He's not coming. But he wants to see you."

Back inside the lab, Thantos and the others were gathered around what was now unquestionably a corpse, and some images on screens. Thantos pulled me over to one of the screens. "Look."

I saw something like a blue x-ray of a man in profile, and on his back something that was a cross between an octopus and maybe a 3-foot long mosquito. "That's it. The parasite."

"Its huge… who is this a photo of?"

Thantos looked at the body on the gurney. "Charlie here. We snapped this picture with an Electroscopic camera at the same time we sent 50,000 volts through his body. The parasite lit up the x-ray spectrum. This is proof, Tyson. Proof that we are not crazy."

"But you killed a man, Thantos."

Thantos looked at me with a odd blankness that made me remember what Helena said earlier. In that moment he was no more than a corpse himself. Animated, perhaps, but dead all the same. I could feel it, the *absence*, just like she said. "It wasn't the first thing we tried, Tyson. We didn't kill him on purpose, its just what happened."

Dr. Strauss saw me starting to back away and stopped me. "We need you to take Charlie with you" she said.

"I'll pick him up and dispose of the body in a couple of days," Thantos added, "just leave him in your trunk."

I was speechless.

"It's necessary that you move the body for, you know, legal reasons. Helena will understand. Nobody will come for him, don't worry, he was Donna's nephew and has no other family."

I guess I must have nodded some kind ascent, because William the Fat and Donna were wheeling the gurney out to the car before I knew it. Donna rolled the body bag into the trunk with less care than I take with a sack of potatoes.

Thantos leaned in and whispered, "Soon, we'll be able to kill them. Don't worry." He must have seen alarm in my face. "The parasites," he added.

Neither Helena nor I spoke at all on the drive home. Every police car made us tense. Every bump in the road reminded us of our unwelcome cargo. Things had definitely taken a dark turn.

Orpheus

She insisted we go to church. We needed to pray, she said. This was stated as a non-negotiable fact, so I went. I followed her lead in the kneeling and genuflections, but was frankly moved only by the sight of her being moved. We are curious creatures, humans. A thing can be made real to us by the mere fact that it is real to someone we care about. If this ritual had the power to affect Helena, then it had power. That I did not understand it or feel it outside of her presence made vanishing little difference. I had come to know in the past weeks how little I knew of not just the world, but my own self and mind. That I was in any way qualified to judge the value of metaphysical divinities was patently obvious.

Still, it was clear that I was outside my comfort zone. "Thanks for doing this," she said afterwards, "I know you didn't have to or want to."

"I'm not religious, no."

"Neither am I, not in the doctrine sort of way. I like the space, the sound, the feeling I get being in there. It's a place where its okay to be quiet and serious and alone with your thoughts. I think the soul needs that. The Orphic belief is that the body only holds the soul for a short while, and when it dies the soul finds a new companion, and on and on, until the time it can be free. Our jobs are to nurture it, provide for it, let it grow. I think that at, once upon a time, all our souls were connected through God, and now they are all disconnected, each as part of a person, but that one day we will all be joined together again." She fell silent for a moment, and I was momentarily filled with a warm joy at the sound of all our souls being united.

But only for a moment, because I then thought of how I would be sharing Helena with countless others in a cloud of bliss, but an undifferentiated cloud of bliss, and how really, what

I wanted was to have this bliss be specific, have it be between me and her and not anybody else. To be together alone, was that wrong? Ungenerous?

"But I don't know about Thantos," she whispered, "I think maybe he is lost." She renewed then her commitment to go south, get out of Texas, and find spiritual nourishment with or without Thantos.

I promised again to go with her with all the wild abandon in my heart, but it sounded off, it sounded hollow. I was hearing the words come out and at the same time wondering if I was telling the truth. But why would I doubt my resolve? I spent a week struggling to find any accommodations and paid three times what the Waldorf Astoria costs for the privilege of pitching a tent in a hayfield. I knew I would struggle with this for days. I always did. If Thantos was out of the picture, if it was just her and me, wouldn't that be exactly what I wanted?

A moment here to explain something about this trip to Jacinto, Mexico. It was a complete lark. We just randomly picked the place out of the blue. There is nothing particularly going on right now, nor any particular tourist hotspots there. We weren't even interested in the coastal area, we wanted to go to the central plains. Nobody should want to go there, really, which is precisely why we chose it initially. I could not, apparently, have been more wrong. Booking flights through Orbitz or any online vendor was completely impossible. When I called travel agents, the first two laughed out loud when I told them where I wanted to go. We would have to drive. But even lodgings, anywhere in the entire state of Jacinto were impossible to find at any price. Farmers and ranchers were renting out woodsheds and makeshift "campsites" in cow pastures. The rumor was that some kind of enormous festival was happening, some kind of folk concert and spiritual "happening". But it was impossible to find anyone who had any firm details, but tens of thousands of people were descending there nonetheless. Drawn there, called there. Just like us.

As promised, Thantos appeared in two days at my house and took away the body of the experiment. He was elated at the progress they were making regarding the parasites.

"Now that you know," he asked in a secretive manner, as if somehow whispering kept the parasite from hearing, "what does it feel like? Can you feel it on you? Does it weigh anything? It probably doesn't weigh anything, it has no mass we can detect, but it has to do something to you, right? Can you tell?"

"Aside from the nausea I feel when you describe it? No, Thantos, sorry. I would rather assume you are insane than right, if you don't mind."

"There's something else. We figured out, I think, why the cancer treatment was discontinued. We managed to recreate the type of radiation beam, and did some experiments."

My stomach clenched at the word *experiment*.

"It kills them. Fries them right off the subject's body."

"I don't understand the connection."

"Is it not obvious? The parasites got scared, they thought up a plan and did something. Its pretty clear they can change what people want to do, they sensed a threat and made it go away."

"What do you mean they thought? They are octopus bugs that are invisible and they *think*? They have *plans*?"

"Seems like it. They saw this as a problem and made everybody forget about it. Makes sense from their point of view."

"I guess."

I had to let the creepiness of this settle down a bit. Its one thing to be told you have a grotesque invisible jellyfish living on your back. Its quite another to think that it's as smart as you are and hatching "plans" while it sits back there. And that it can make you carry them out.

"So, the experiment, is he…"

"She is fine. No harm at all. No side effects, unless you count her sudden clarity of thought."

"You can do it then. You can get rid of the parasite and it works?"

"Yes. We can get rid of yours, let you see the things its keeping you from seeing."

"She can see the dots and whale now?"

"Just like the rest of us."

"When? When can you do it?"

Frankly I surprised myself. Five minutes earlier I would have said that gruesome laboratory was the last place on earth I would ever go again. But something about the thought of being a puppet to a parasite shook me up more than I care to admit. I wasn't *entirely* convinced I had a giant phantom bug thing on my back, but I had spent a lifetime being conflicted, confused, muddle headed, and hesitating at every turn. I had already lost one wife and was so lacking in resolve that I would no doubt lose Helena before I even had her. Doubt was my middle name. If that could be made to go away, if I could have a single lucid view of my future, well, then what would be lost? But my mention of the dots had darkened Thantos' face. His giddiness had evaporated.

"It doesn't really matter at all I suppose, if we are all dead in a week anyway. Humans, parasites, all of it. We all perish together when that thing hits us."

No. No. No. I couldn't lose my doubts at the very moment it became meaningless. "How are you sure? Nobody can see it."

Thantos sighed a deep sigh of resignation. He wasn't happy about knowing this. "It has an enormous electromagnetic signature that's easy enough to see, even if it cant be seen with the naked eye. It's a hundred times bigger than the one that killed the dinosaurs."

"And its going to hit us for sure?"

"Yeah, it should." I stared at him, and he shifted around a bit uncharacteristically. When it came to his science mumbo-jumbo, he was always sure.

"Okay, well, don't tell the others this, okay?"

"Tell them what?"

"It doesn't have a very stable course. It sort of… hesitates… a bit."

"The asteroid *hesitates?*"

"I can't really explain it, but it seems to slow down and go a bit off course and then there will be an abrupt correction… the overall trajectory is the same, but..." he kept on talking, sinking into some deeper astronomical blabber about parabolas and inertia, but I had stopped really listening.

Because suddenly, I could explain it. The whole shebang emerged from the fuzzy cloud of my head. It started with the asteroid. It wasn't just hurtling toward the earth by chance. This was no ordinary lump of space rock on a random collision course. No. Randomness does not hesitate, it careens boldly. This asteroid had purpose. This asteroid was in love. Romeo gave his life to join Juliet in heaven. Orpheus descended to hell itself to rescue his wife Eurydice. And this asteroid, alternately uncertain and determined, was coming to earth, in search of a lost love.

Leviathan

This long lost love, however, was also sadly long dead. Centuries, perhaps millennia dead. The asteroid would find only a graveyard.

The great whale Leviathan, in ancient lore, was said to be not only an immortal monster that no man could hope to kill or injure, but also the living Hellmouth, luring souls through a sweet temptation into its massive yaw from which there was no return. He was both a beast and a passageway to eternal damnation. Until that final day of judgement when God would

smash the great creature to bits and return all the souls to
heaven.

I now know, with the furious light of madness I know it,
that this impossible colossus was not only real, and beyond even
the wildest descriptions that men in their puny imaginations
were able to set to words, but that its eternal remains are lying a
thousand kilometers under San Jacinto, Mexico. And I know
where hell is for the tormented souls that it carried within. It is
here. It is us. The Leviathan, vast and generous, did not steal
souls from humans, but carried with it countless numbers of the
phantasmal octopus creatures we call the parasites through
boundless and endless eons of space and time until it perished,
here, on our cold little rock. Where once the millions of
creatures lived off one enormous consciousness, now they were
scattered, fending for themselves to find some tiny miserable
creature to affix to. How lonely they must be, after knowing the
vast glory of a creature whose body disappeared beyond the
horizon in both directions, now curled over a puny man little
bigger than yourself. Such solitude! It is no wonder at all that
they yearned to be reunited, yearned for that moment to return
to the heavens where their great mother sailed. And now we are
called home. *We?* No, not we, *they.*

But. Why did I suddenly know this? What had happened?

I now believe that some combination of my thoughts and urges, perhaps the sudden decision to subject myself to the treatment, led to an abrupt change in my relationship with what I slowly grew to accept was my attached incorporeal companion. I'm still working it out. If it is there, or rather here, then what it wants and fears is not always clear. Its hard to tell where it ends and I begin, to be honest. But I have knowledge that I did not have before, could not have ever had before, and this part I know is either from my creature or something of mine that my creature is now letting me see for the first time for reasons of its own. If this is true, then its not only not just a mindless jelly bug, it not only has simple survival plans like a dog might have plans to retrieve a bone; no, this thing has actual sentience, it has a mind.

Somehow, through combination of my own thoughts and the delirium-like daydreams that the creature provided, I came to the conclusion that if I just waited until after Helena and I went to Jalisco, all would be solved. The spiritual renewal that she spoke of was in fact the freeing of us from the parasites. Leviathan may have perished here countless years ago, but she was not alone in this universe. Where there is one, there is another, and it was coming. And we could go home with her. No. No, not we, *they*. Only they. They.

But that was days ago. Now its no longer coming. Now it has come. And it has gone. I'm in Jalisco, finally. I found her.

Not my car though, alas. It was complete chaos for hundreds of miles. I had never seen so many people and cars in my life, tangled in a confused knot without end. Now the two of us are on the bus again, and we are heading home. Thantos' fears of the end of the world were overblown. The vast creature was ultimately as incorporeal as the parasites themselves and passed gently right through the earth, pausing to ruminate a moment as it slowly swam through the embers of a lost mate, and moving on. It caused no visible physical damage at all.

But when I came to accept the reality of my companion, of the succubus that clung to me and used me and that I abhorred, I came to understand something about this horrible battle of the mind, how from this torment and self-loathing and doubt comes the sublime nature of the human spirit. I saw this as clearly as I saw what the purely rational minds of the invisibles were capable of when stripped of this second voice, this seemingly unreasonable pull in directions of the heart and gut that bind these creatures, and thus us, together. And I saw this as something that, perhaps irrationally, I was afraid to lose after all. And strange as it sounds, I think that my greed to have Helena to myself resonated with my companion, for I had no more visions of Mexico, or warm climes.

The night before we were scheduled to leave I told Helena that we couldn't go. That I wouldn't. I didn't tell her why exactly, because I'm not sure I could even have explained it yet, even if she believed me at all. But I knew that what I loved of her were the questions she had deep in her eyes, the tumult of her dreams and her need of the poets and quiet empty spaces. She was the unknown I craved, and the unknown does not exist in certitude. I was more afraid of losing the questions, than of the questions themselves. She didn't have a car, and there was no other reasonable way to go, so I figured that was end of it. If we stayed put, nothing would change, and that was as it should be.

But in the morning I found that she had taken my car and gone without me. Her urge to go was too strong, and I was a fool to not know it. It was the worst of all possible worlds. I had to either stop her, or join her. I tried my best, but the bus was so slow, traffic was backed up for hours and hours.

I failed. When I eventually arrived, when I looked upon the thousands of people walking past me in all directions, I saw them with my eyes, heard them with my ears, counted them with my mind, but something indefinable about them was just as I feared. The impossibly cavernous, irresistible mouth of Leviathan had passed this way.

Now, finally, heading back home with eighteen hours of monotonous rumbling to look forward to, we are together again. But I am nonetheless still alone. More alone, undeniably, than before. I look into her eyes and they are lovely and serene, but I know only half of her looks back. The flesh half, the part that shares most of its DNA with an industrious and clear purposed squirrel. The unknowable mystery is... absent. As for me, I am severed, adrift. The cord tying me to her has come unraveled, the anchor gone. I am two halves, I know that now more than ever, but a single careless mistake has left both halves abandoned, empty, and at the threshold of a newly strange and repulsive land. Romeo would render himself onto the angels, Orpheus would descend to Hades. But for Mr. Welles, the boring English teacher, and his wretched ethereal companion, heaven and hell both have come and gone, and only the dry, inevitable earth remains.

The Astrolabio Amoris

The exhibit at the Franklin Institute, named *Charlatans and their Machines*, featured nearly a hundred devices from various eras that were claimed to be capable of any number of things from curing consumption, restoring eyesight, straightening the spine, and even arresting the aging process. It was due to open in two weeks when the final shipment of artifacts arrived from Wilhelm Reich museum. Aside from the expected Orgone machines and Cloudbuster apparatus, there was included a device labeled "Unknown Artifact (Astrolabio?)"

This Astrolabio was a machine that came into the possession of the museum as part of the Reich estate, but was, as far as anyone could ascertain, something he had acquired from someone else. The Reich museum included it in the shipment because it was an odd looking device that had been sitting in their basement, but they had no clue as to its function, use, or origins.

Jeremy Gillespie, however, immediately recognized the small engraved "RPL" on one of the machine's many parts as the initials of Roger Poinze Laboratories, the bogus company of one Beatrice "Roger" Poinze, a 19th century adherent of Mesmer who had carved out her own tiny niche in the vast world of quakery. As a woman engineer of dubious machines, she presented herself at all times as Roger Poinze's secretary and assistant, who met the public while the "real" Roger Poinze was indisposed or overseas, which was always the case.

Jeremy was just an assistant at the exhibition, a hired temporary laborer, but the only one that had heard of Beatrice Poinze. The machine, lacking context or description, was relegated to the basement just as it had languished for generations in other basements. Jeremy, however, had spent years collecting odd trivia about love potions, aphrodisiacs and magical enchantments to lure the object of one's affections. Being neither an attractive nor particularly charming person, and seeing his thirtieth birthday inexorably approaching without any visible signs of ever finding romance, he had turned increasingly to fanciful, to not say wishful, methods of courtship, and hence to the writings of Beatrice "Roger" Poinze.

Although not particularly talented, Jeremy had all the more unfortunate trappings of an artist. He was volatile, undisciplined, explosive and passionate, but all to little effect or result. He was a random event, pinballing through time, creating havoc. One day he was a poet, the next a painter, then a filmmaker, then a trash-artist, only to reverse course and denounce all art, burn all that he had made and leave chaos as his only gift to the few people that reluctantly accepted him as a friend. He would refuse to eat, then binge, get impossibly sick, blame his friends for mistreating him, enroll in school, drop out, and then begin writing poetry again, begging his friends for forgiveness. He would be constantly moving from apartment to apartment, and job to job, selling all his possessions only to begin buying nearly identical ones a few months later. All of this without the benefit of any drug habit whatsoever. All of this was the natural Jeremy.

This destructive cycle of behavior was such that no sane person could be around for very long, let alone a potential girlfriend. Certainly he attracted a particular kind of girl periodically, the kind that was equally turbulent and frenzied, but this would only last a night, maybe a weekend, before they flew apart in separate directions. None of these girls had ever fit, none had understood him or been willing to stick around to even try, they were just sharing the same roller coaster car for a couple of days before going separately toward other rides. He did not deny that it may be his fault, but it was unclear what he could do about it. Certainly he could not be so very bizarre that not a single woman in the world would want him. There had to be somebody that could figure him out and think it worthwhile to do so. Beatrice Poinze had offered that sort of hope. She had written that it was *inevitable* that every person had a perfect mate. She not only promised this hope, she guaranteed it.

Poinze had taken to heart the teachings of Franz Mesmer regarding magnetic fields present in humans and animals and carried it forward to the new and exciting field of "magneto-electric harmonizing." Her Harmonizers were reported to be devices capable of "tuning" the magnetic fields of couples such that they would be more synchronized, and thus increasing domestic bliss, and, importantly, "leading to the increase of the sensual passions and potencies." Moreover, and more significantly for Jeremy, she claimed to have a created a method for locating one's perfect mate via the use of electro-magnetic energies alone.

"This new apparatus, the only one of its kind in the world, uses the initiating subjects magnetic resonance to locate an exact anti-pole, a perfectly synchronized and thus ideal counterpart across all time and space for any subject" read the description on one of Poinze's many promotional pieces for her services. "There is no such thing as a magnetic field with only one pole, so if a subject is the positive, there must exist, somewhere, that person's negative. If there is a north, it only exists because there also exists a south. It cannot be otherwise."

This was the holy grail for Jeremy Gillespie, the notion that a machine could find anybody's ideal match, the one person who would "harmonize" with his own strange idiosyncrasies and not only tolerate, but enjoy them. This machine she called the *Astrolabio Amoris*, the astrolabe of love, and it now stood before Jeremy Gillespie in the basement of the Franklin Institute.

The machine was in remarkably good condition. It appeared to have been hardly used at all, and well stored. While Jeremy was no scientist or engineer, he was impressed by the complexity and intricacy of the device. From his own collection of Poinze's pamphlets he was able to find a number of illustrations of the machine and some descriptions of its workings, so that within the week he had successfully assembled the device.

According to Poinze, the device was powered entirely by the "natural magnetic currents flowing between subjects." The first part of the machine included a small stool for the "initiating subject." As Jeremy sat on the stool, it pushed down on a piston that caused a dozen thin metal antennas to extend toward his body and head. These probes, and also a surrounding "Æther Screen" were connected to the main portion of the machine that resembled a supercharged crystal radio. Countless tightly wound copper wire coils and arrays of foil "magneto-receivers" all culminating in the "Tele-Photonic Imager" which translated the magnetic current to a visible image. In fact, it was a blurry blob that began to glow on the "imager" when he sat down, but the machine had a "Magneto-Iris Focus" knob that, with a few turns, brought a startlingly lifelike face into view. Not a still image or video projection, but something resembling the image of a camera obscura, entirely alive and of the moment. This was the face destined for Jeremy Gillespie.

The device, incredibly, actually worked. Jeremy could not have been more shocked if an elephant in a tutu had flown out from the middle of the jumbled wires and brass fittings. He stared dumbfounded at this lovely, incredible girl's face on the milky glass plate of the imager. She had short spiky hair and alert, intelligent, eyes. Panicking that this image would not last, Jeremy pulled out his phone and shot a stream of ten virtually identical pictures. Quickly he also photographed the MagnetoCompass direction and the reading on the AutoSpatial Estimator. These two indicators gave him an approximate direction and distance from his current whereabouts to his perfect match.

Was it a coincidence that she was only a few miles north? Of all the places in the world? Or was it inevitable that his perfect counterpart would share a geographic history? He thought he was sick of this lousy city and its stodgy history. He thought he wanted to leave it with all the madness in his soul to find something new and energizing. He had hoped that his ideal mate might be in Copenhagen, or Athens, or some other exotic land, but was he really, deep down, so tied to this place that only someone equally attached to Philly would ever possibly be his soul mate?

He checked the directions, and headed off before she had a chance to leave. He didn't have a name or any other way to find her if he did not act now. As it turned out, he came to the Greenline Café within fifteen minutes.

His girl, however, was not there.

He showed her picture to one of the waitresses. She told him it sort of looked like a girl that came in but she couldn't be sure, so he made a point to stop at the café as often as possible, and eventually, a couple of days later, he spotted her. It was actually very difficult to be sure. Her hair was long and drawn back in a ponytail, quite unlike what he had seen in the machine, and she hid behind a laptop. But while so many of the collected slackers and graduate students slumped and frumped at their tables, this girl was ramrod straight, her eyes electric. The eyes and posture gave her away.

He went up to her table. Introduced himself as a lonely poet and artist, sat down and waited for the magic to happen.

She glanced at him nervously for a few moments, then pulled some bills out of her wallet, placed them under her coffee cup, snapped her laptop shut, stood up, said, "Nice meeting you" and walked away. Briskly. Clearly Poinze's machine was not going to do all the work for him.

For the next week, Jeremy professed his love in a multitude of ways, from a hideously rendered painting in acrylics to hastily written poetry and even extending to an inedible heart shaped cake he had the waitress present to her. It went from bad to worse.

Emily, which was the extent of the information he had managed to gather, was not in the least interested in him nor in any crazy "artist," even if he had been a good one. As it turns out, she was deeply involved in programming and logic, and in creating models and simulations with complex differential equations. She was as sharp and smart as Jeremy was scattershot and emotional. But Jeremy trusted Beatrice Poinze and her inscrutable machine. He had to. He had tried just about everything else over the years, and this was the first time he felt that someone was *destined* to love him. Maybe not right away, but eventually, and permanently, and blissfully.

By the end of that second week, he came to realize what had to happen. This was the girl for him. That was established fact. If she didn't see it yet, then he just needed to step up his game. If she was his match, then clearly he had not prepared himself all these years and he had to make up for lost time. So as only an overwrought madman can, he plunged headfirst into making himself the person he had to be. Reinvention was his only real constant, purging the past his greatest skillset, and delusional confidence in his success his unflagging source of propulsion. Creating the right Jeremy Gillespie was just another form of art, an enormous, immersive performance, but one he had been preparing for since adolescence.

It was neither quick nor painless, but Jeremy slowly, methodically, twisted his life around. He enrolled, for the fourth time, in community college. This time, with a tangible goal in mind, he stuck to it. He concentrated not on exotic arts, but on those things that Emily seemed to value: mathematics, logic, programming, statistics. These were, for Jeremy, far more esoteric than the *Sturm und Drang* choices he had made in the past. Startlingly, these ideas, this forced discipline, this path of dry data manipulation did not repulse him as he had assumed all his life. On the contrary, the more he involved himself in it, the more it pulled him in. In this, in the workings of formulas, algorithms and plain logical proofs, he began to find a calmness and serenity he had rarely known. In this world, in Emily's world, there was the possibility of actual certainty. The same certainty of Poinze's machine, a mechanical set of truisms for the functioning of the world. It was plainly seductive for a catastrophic mess like Jeremy.

He knew the process would not be a short one, she had years on him, but slowly as the semesters passed he found he could occasionally broach a subject at the café that made him sound momentarily intelligent and warranted a response from her. He hit on the idea of asking for her advice and help on difficult problems and by the end of two years they were not only speaking regularly at the café, but she would actually expect him there at least once a week with some problem he was working on.

He surprised himself by then applying to the University of Pennsylvania, where Emily herself was finishing a doctorate, to continue his studies. When he was accepted, and he began his upper division classes, he was three years into his plan, and he was without a doubt an entirely different person. More than this, the performance had transformed the performer. He now looked back at the raw, undisciplined character he was a few years ago and could not fully grasp what he was thinking, how he could have lived like a tornado. His life now was a model of steadfastness, order and direction. Any day now, Emily would see him as the perfect match he already knew he was. He had reached and passed the age of thirty, but no longer with dread, for now it was clear what was ahead and it was good.

But as the days and weeks went on, something else was at work. Emily's appearances at the café became more erratic and irregular. Her impeccable attire showed signs of carelessness. Her focus on the final stages of her dissertation, now finally within her grasp, seemed to wander and drift, as if concluding it had become a chore and not the delight it had been before.

Finally, one day, she appeared at the café and sat down next to Jeremy, who was working out some code longhand with a legal pad. When he looked up, he was startled to see her. She had chopped off her hair. The luxurious waves that flowed down her back were gone, replaced by a boyish pixie cut. Next to her, a gigantic camping pack.

"I'm leaving" she told him, "Kate spent her entire life getting ready to be something, getting ready to start her great adventure. She never went to Europe even. I'm done. No more waiting."

Jeremy had known for some time that Emily had a sister, Kate, who had been studying law. The two of them were really close, they shared everything. He asked her what she was talking about. Her eyes almost burned a hole in his skull. She said Kate was dead. She had suffered an aneurism, collapsed in the library, and never woke up.

"There's no logic. None of that" she said, poking at his lines of code, "amounts to anything. The world is fucking chaos.

I'm just going. I have some money, and this pack, and the rest of it can rot for all I care."

Jeremy was frozen with confusion. "Where?" he finally sputtered, "I mean, are you going?"

She didn't know. She didn't care. She hoped to get on a boat or the cheapest plane ride across the ocean. It didn't matter. She had thrown her entire dissertation and her laptop into the trash and said she never wanted to see it again. She and her sister had been saving themselves, just as soon as they finished they would head out into the world, and that dissertation, those years, had been all the time they actually had. She had traded life for paper. She was not happy with her choice. She wanted nothing to do with that path any longer.

"So you want to come with me?"

"But, where?"

"Does it matter? You want to come or not? I'm heading to the station right now."

And she left. Briskly and sharply down the sidewalk, an enormous pack towering over her small frame. They had exchanged a few more confused words, but, in the end, Jeremy was incapable of just dropping everything like Emily. He had things he wanted to do, needed to do. He was in the middle of so many profound discoveries. He couldn't just spin on a dime.

Chuck it all out. Could he? Maybe once, perhaps, he could. Not, however, anymore.

He sat at the café for a long time wondering what had just happened. Why he was here alone suddenly, floundering in midstream, looking out to where his destination had been, where his lighthouse had shone clearly just minutes before, only to see nothing. It was gone.

He pulled out his phone as he had done periodically over the last few years and looked at the photos he had taken that day while seated on the *Astrolabis Amoris*. The glowing face on the milky plate that was his best, only, true companion. He stared at those pictures and wondered how he had never figured this out before.

All this time he had wondered why that amazing contraption had not brought Beatrice Poinze fame and fortune. Why she had committed suicide at such a young age. But it was perfectly clear why, and why the machine had been so rarely used. If only he had read a little more carefully.

"A perfectly synchronized and thus ideal counterpart across all *time* and space..."

The Warning Tube

That blank look of bafflement, the one that you can see isn't firing a single neuron or closing a single synapse, that's the one I fear most. With that one look, that vacant, uncomprehending stare, a door slowly closes on an entire part of my life. And here it was again.

It wasn't the first time. I've closed a door every few years, creating sealed compartments that hold things once considered so vital and essential to what I thought of as me. Once in a great while I would stumble across evidence of these closed off rooms, usually in the form of some half-forgotten acquaintance I would meet by chance and who would uproariously guffaw "do you remember when we used to..." and I would nod and laugh obligingly but not really recall what or when they found so memorable. I hadn't been in whatever attic they were still inhabiting in so long that its musty contents were but historical relics that filled me not with recognition but with mystery.

When I moved in with Samantha I was intoxicated by the adventure she embodied. She was vivacious, electrifying, full of new ideas and a youthful disregard for consequences that was everything I was not. She opened a door to an enticing new landscape.

Not an empty one, of course. Part of the thrill was that it was full of strange and wonderful things that were Samantha. I assumed that she felt the same about my own peculiar assortment of furnishings now commingling in the room with hers. I exist as the collection of desires, mannerisms, tics, jokes, ideas and behaviors that she must have found interesting in some way. What is revealed quickly enough in a new relationship, however, is that what is liked in each other is the quirky and colorful dresser, the stoic armoire, the ornate desk. But we really have no idea that the drawers in the armoire are full of dirty socks, yellowed porn, or a collection of dead mice preserved in small bottles. This assorted content is arguably the part that counts the most, but you don't go around opening other people's furniture until it becomes also your own furniture.

In any event, it occurred that this morning was the first time in the whirlwind period that had been my weeks with

Samantha that I found myself in our new mutual bathroom using up the last squares of toilet paper on the roll.

This presented an opportunity. Fortuitously enough, the landscape of this apartment was similar to the dumpy old condo I recently shared with my soon-to-be-ex-wife in one maddening respect: a ridiculously minute amount of storage space in the bathroom. So our supply of toilet paper rolls were stored down the hall in the laundry closet, which made running out of toilet paper a dangerous proposition.

So I was eager to initiate Samantha to one of my little rituals, and was looking forward to what would happen next, like a little boy wanting to show off the frog he captured with his father's new hat, when just a few moments later Sam walked by with a new roll of toilet paper in her hand.

"Ah. So you saw it."

She stopped. "Saw what?"

"The Warning Tube."

"The What?"

"The Warning Tube. On the toilet lid."

"What are you talking about?"

"Didn't you see the empty roll standing on the toilet?"

"Yeah."

"That's the Warning Tube. So you don't sit down and start your business before you realize that theres no more TP."

I grinned at her and that's when it happened.

No. More precisely, that's when nothing happened. I was speaking a foreign tongue, showing her a secret compartment in my bedside table that contained, as far as she could tell, little more than crumpled up trash that she would have to throw out in due course. That this sad little pile of litter was the entire remains of five wonderful and hilarious years of matrimony did not register anywhere.

"Whatever," she said, as if speaking to an imbecile on a street corner, "I always check."

And she went into the bathroom, and closed the door.

In Rest, Victory.

When the war against the robots comes, as it must someday, I believe the popular conception that humans will be at a disadvantage is misguided.

A Machine may not be technically alive, but it will fear death in a way humans do not. A robot has no angels at its side, and at the moment when its existence is at the precipice, it will know only the abyss, and it will be afraid. Humans, I realize now, do have angels, and they will make us ultimately stronger.

I would never have professed such a belief even a few short days ago, but now it is completely clear. In particular, the entire mystery of the Angel of Death crystallized in a single moment.

What would ever have caused someone at some distant dark corner of the past to imagine Death as an angel had been one of the many irreconcilable irrationalities that I attributed to the vagaries of mysticism. Angels were not something I could associate with the closing in of the eternal darkness. But then, in one amazing moment, I saw her. I stared into the immaculate face of She Who Gives the Final Kiss and all my fears vanished, and the inescapable doom of the Robots was revealed.

Despite all of their clanking, grinding power and laser guided apparatus; despite all the titanium skins, multiprocessor brains and single-minded purpose, I had done something that no mechanical creature could ever do. I had made, from my own flesh, a small and tiny being that looked up and into my eyes, and I knew then that I had nothing to fear.

One day, this will be the last face I see, and she will make certain that I am carried gently to lovely spot, and will lay me down to rest in the earth. She will guide me through the last final moments and then she will keep the memory of me alive when I am finally gone.

I have brought into this world my own Angel of Death, and she is beautiful.

For Roxanne.

Fini

Thank you for reading.

Contact me at

Publishing@CineFont.com